The Great Bunny Escape

To Jaida
—G. S.

#9

DREAMER

THE GReat BuNNy Escape

By Holly ANNa • Illustrated by Genevieve Santos

LITTLE SIMON
New York   London   Toronto   Sydney   New Delhi

This book is a work of fiction. Any references to historical events, real people, or real places are used fictitiously. Other names, characters, places, and events are products of the author's imagination, and any resemblance to actual events or places or persons, living or dead, is entirely coincidental.

LITTLE SIMON

An imprint of Simon & Schuster Children's Publishing Division

1230 Avenue of the Americas, New York, New York 10020

First Little Simon paperback edition February 2019

Copyright © 2019 by Simon & Schuster, Inc.

Also available in a Little Simon hardcover edition.

All rights reserved, including the right of reproduction in whole or in part in any form.

LITTLE SIMON is a registered trademark of Simon & Schuster, Inc., and associated colophon is a trademark of Simon & Schuster, Inc. For information about special discounts for bulk purchases, please contact Simon & Schuster Special Sales at 1-866-506-1949 or business@simonandschuster.com.

The Simon & Schuster Speakers Bureau can bring authors to your live event. For more information or to book an event contact the Simon & Schuster Speakers Bureau at 1-866-248-3049 or visit our website at www.simonspeakers.com.

Designed by Laura Roode

Manufactured in the United States of America 0119 MTN

2 4 6 8 10 9 7 5 3 1

This book has been cataloged with the Library of Congress.

ISBN 978-1-5344-2655-9 (pbk)

ISBN 978-1-5344-2656-6 (hc)

ISBN 978-1-5344-2657-3 (eBook)

CONTENTS

☆ Chapter One ☆

A Secret and a Favor

BRRRING!

The school bell rings, and my best friends, Lily and Jasmine, and I make a mad dash for the playground. It's recess! Our favorite time of the day. *Obviously.*

We hit the blacktop and run straight to the Hideout—our top secret hiding spot under the slide.

It's the best place for telling secrets because it keeps all the snoopy-snoops like Gabby Gaburp and Carol Rattinger out.

Today Lily has a *huge* secret. I can tell because she always twirls her hair around her finger when she's hiding something. And she's been twirling her hair ALL. DAY. LONG.

"Spill, Lil!" I say as soon as we're safe inside the Hideout.

"Let's make extra sure the coast is clear first," Lily says. So Jasmine double-checks the entry to make sure Carol and Gabby aren't spying on us. You can never be too careful when it comes to those two girls. They want to know *everything* about *everyone*.

"All clear!" Jasmine calls.

"Okay," Lily begins. "You may have already guessed I have a secret to tell, and I also have a favor to ask."

That sounds like a double-dog secret! I think, scootching closer to her side. And I am double-dog interested.

"First the secret," Lily says. She pauses to build the suspense. Then she spills. "I'm going on a *cruise!*" And we all squeal at the same time.

"My *whole* family is going," Lily continues. "And there's going to be a pool, a water slide, a movie theater, and dance parties *every night!*"

"WOW!" Jasmine exclaims. "That will be *awesome!*"

Lily claps her hands excitedly and cheers, "A whole *week* of awesome!"

Then Lily takes a deep breath and looks at Jasmine and me with total puppy-dog eyes. "But now I have to ask the favor," she says. "Can one of you take care of my bunny, Cutie Pie, while I'm away?"

Jasmine's already shaking her head. "I better not," she says. "I'm not good with rabbits, and rabbits are not good with me. One time wild rabbits ate my entire vegetable garden. They're sneaky little critters."

Then Lily turns to me, and I already know my answer.

"I would *love* to take care of Cutie Pie," I say. "But I have to ask my mom first."

The three of us wriggle out of the Hideout to go find my mom, who happens to be a teacher at my school, which is pretty handy. *Obviously.* My mom is in her classroom, so I ask if I can take care of Cutie Pie for a whole week.

Mom closes her book slowly and asks, "Do you think you can handle it, Daisy?"

I hippity-hop up and down like a rabbit and say, "I *know* I can handle it!"

Then my mom says Y.E.S.

Lily, Jasmine, and I are *all* hopping up and down now, because I get to be an official bunny babysitter!

Ga-boing! Ga-boing! Ga-boing!

☆ Chapter Two ☆

Rabbit Rules

Ding-Dong!

I peek out my bedroom window, and it's *them*! I gallop down the stairs like a wild racehorse all the way to the front door. Lily's dad holds a huge cage in his arms. Inside the cage I can see a fluffy white bunny with a cotton ball tail. No wonder his name is Cutie Pie. He is *so cute.*

I invite Lily, her dad, and Cutie Pie inside. Then I sneak a peek at the cage and see Cutie Pie sniff-sniff-sniffing with his cute little nose.

Lily's Dad carries everything to my bedroom. Lily and I hop up the stairs one by one and then scamper down the hall after him.

When we get to my room, Lily tells me how to care for her bunny. She even gives me a list of rabbit rules, which we go over together.

The Rules of Rabbit Ownership
by Lily

1. Hay Feeder should always be full.
2. Replace water every day.
3. Provide a few fresh greens daily, like broccoli, cabbage, celery leaves, dandelions, or kale.
4. Serve 1 tablespoon of rabbit pellets each day.
5. Clean wet litter and add fresh litter as needed.
6. Let rabbit roam outside the cage daily. WATCH CAREFULLY!
7. Cuddle and pet. ♡
8. Play with your rabbit! Rabbits love to play!
9. Provide cardboard for your rabbit to chew on.

Wow, I think. Rabbits are a lot of work!

Then Lily realizes she forgot Cutie Pie's snacks and toys in the car.

"I'll go and get them," she says, and sprints out of my room.

And now it's time to introduce myself to Cutie Pie. "Hello, little bunny."

Cutie Pie watches me with his pink gemlike eyes.

"Do you want to have fun with me this week?" I ask.

He twitches his pink nose and says, "I always want to have fun with *you*, Daisy!"

Whoa! I jump back from the cage like I got zapped by electricity. *Did Cutie Pie just talk to me? I ask myself. Of course not! Rabbits can't talk!*

So then I look around my room . . . and surprise, surprise. Guess who is standing right behind me?

Posey! My imaginary friend. I should have known! *Obviously.*

Chapter Three

Sneeze Attack

"Who is *that*?" Posey asks, peering over my shoulder. He watches Cutie Pie scamper into a tunnel.

"That is Cutie Pie the bunny," I say. "And I'm taking care of him while Lily's on vacation."

Posey races toward the cage to get a closer look. Then his face squinches like he might sneeze.

"That sounds like a lot of *fff* . . . *fff* . . . *fff* . . . *fun!*" His face relaxes again. "May I introduce myself?"

"Sure!" I tell him. *What harm can it do?*

Posey presses his face against the cage. "Hello, Cutie Pie! My name is Po . . . Po . . . Po . . . ."

Then Posey erupts like a goopy volcano. *"ACHOOO!"*

A mist of glitter gook sprays from his mouth and nose and showers all over my room! Whoa, my imaginary friend has glitter boogers! I want to scream *Ew!* and *Wow!* at the same time.

"Sorry!" Posey says as the glittery goo spatters *everything* in my room.

He scrunches his nose again, and this time I *duck*.

"*ACHOOO!*" Posey zooms backward and flies right through the door to the World of Make-Believe, which he left open. A few moments later he peeks back inside my room.

"Bless you!" I say, even though I kind of want to say *Gross*, because my room is completely covered in glitter boogers. "What am I supposed to do about all this shiny mess?"

Posey's nose is still twitching like he might sneeze again.

"I said I was sorry!" he tells me as
the next sneeze—*thankfully*—passes.
Then Posey trots back into my room.

I sigh.

"Well, at least you
didn't glitter-blast
Cutie Pie," I say.
Then I turn to look
in the cage, and that's
when I do a double take.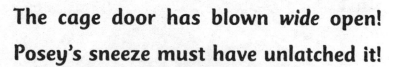
The cage door has blown *wide* open!
Posey's sneeze must have unlatched it!

I check all the hiding spots in the cage, but it is *totally empty*. I've been bunnysitting for five minutes, and I've already *lost* Lily's bunny!

"Oh no!" I cry. "We have to find Cutie Pie! Lily will be back any minute, and she'll never go on her vacation if she finds out her bunny is missing!"

Posey and I
search my room
upside down and
inside out. We look
under my bed, behind
my desk, and in between the
curtains. But Cutie Pie is
absolutely nowhere.

"Well, at least
I'm not sneezing
anymore,"
Posey says,
rubbing
his nose.

And all I can do is roll my eyes, and that's, of course, when I see Cutie Pie hop right by us.

"STOP!" I shout, lunging for the bunny. But I'm not fast enough.

Boing! Boing! Boing!

Cutie Pie hops right into the WOM!

☆ Chapter Four ☆

The Marshmallow Forest

"After that bunny!" I shout, running through the magic door. Then I look over my shoulder. Posey is walking in slow motion like this whole thing is no big whoop. But it is a big whoop. It's a *giant* big whoop! Because I am responsible for Lily's bunny!

Then a sneaky little hopper hops on the path ahead of us. *Oh, thank goodness!*

"Come here, you big cutie!" I call after him. And for a teeny-tiny second I think this might just be the easiest bunny rescue mission ever. But then . . .

"ACHOOO!"

Posey sneezes another gigantic, glittery sneeze. And before I can even say *Nab that rabbit!* Cutie Pie hops away into a forest.

I stare in through the trees and wait for Posey. He stops beside me and sniffle-snorts.

"I think I might be allergic to your new friend," he says.

Obviously, I think.

"Well, we can't worry about that right now," I say. "We have to find Cutie Pie." As I move to run into the forest, Posey grabs my hand.

"Wait!" he says. "We better not go in there. I've heard it's not a *normal* forest."

I stop and wonder, *Is there anything normal in the World of Make-Believe?*

Then I turn to Posey. "So what kind of forest is it?" I ask a little impatiently.

Posey's eyes grow wide, and he says, "It's the *Marshmallow* Forest."

The Marshmallow Forest? I think. That doesn't sound scary at all. It sounds delicious. I squint at the trees to see if they're loaded with marshmallows, but I can't see any from here.

I shake my head and say, "It doesn't matter what kind of forest this is—I have to find Cutie Pie or Lily will never speak to me again."

Posey frowns. He is very nervous.

"Why don't we just find Lily a *new* pet?" he suggests. Then Posey stoops down and picks up a swirly purple-and-white rock. "I bet she would love a pet that never runs away . . . like a pet rock?"

He holds the rock out in front of me, and I push it away.

"Have you got rocks in your head?" I ask. "Finding Lily a new pet would be like me saying I should just find a new imaginary friend!"

Posey's eyebrows shoot straight up. I can tell he does not want me to find a new imaginary friend.

"Okay, okay," he says. "Let's find that bunny!" Then he runs into the Marshmallow Forest. I hurry after him and notice he's still holding the rock.

"Posey? Are you going to keep that rock as a pet?" I ask.

My imaginary friend looks lovingly at the rock.

"Yes," he says. "And I'm going to name her Shelly."

☆ Chapter Five ☆

It Makes Scents

I sniff the air. The Marshmallow Forest smells amazing . . . like honey, vanilla, and maple syrup all at the same time!

"Where is that smell coming from?" I ask dreamily.

Posey, who is glued to my side, looks up at me. "The trees," he says.

Then I walk up to a tree and look into its leafy branches.

"And what makes this place so dangerous?" I ask.

Posey repeats his answer. "The *trees*."

Honestly, the trees don't look dangerous to me, so I reach out and touch one with my finger. I spring backward. It doesn't feel like a regular tree. It feels like I just touched a person! *That's weird*, I think.

Then a shadow darts across the treetops, and Posey leaps into my arms.

"What was that?" he yells into my ear a billion times too loudly.

I try to regain my balance, but Posey won't loosen his grip on me.

"It was probably just a squirrel," I say.

Though, I have to admit, I have the strangest feeling we're being watched.

Finally Posey lets go of me and slides back to the ground.

"Okay," I say, trying not to let this yummy-smelling forest distract me. "Let's make a plan to find Cutie Pie."

We go into thinking mode. Posey taps the side of his head with his finger, and I squeeze my chin.

"I wonder what smells good to a rabbit," I say.

Posey stops tapping his head and snaps his fingers. "I know!" he says. "Carrots!"

Then he digs in his bottomless pockets and pulls out two carrots that are big and orange. He carries a lot of random stuff in there.

"Want one?" he asks, holding a carrot in my direction. I take it, and we begin to walk while holding the carrots out in front of us.

"Here, *bunny, bunny, bunny!*" we call. "Come and get a crunchy orange carrot!" We wait for an answer and then call again.

This time somebody answers, but it is *not* Cutie Pie.

"Oh, I would love a carrot, *I would!*" says a voice from the forest.

Posey jumps into my arms again. At the same time, a branch from the tree above us reaches down and plucks the carrot right out of my hand!

Posey screams, jumps out of my arms, and sprints away. I freeze and stare at the tree that stole my carrot.

And right before my eyes, a face forms on the tree trunk.

Oh my gosh! I think. *These trees are ALIVE! And they like carrots! And they can TALK!* Then I wonder, *Have they seen Cutie Pie?*

"Posey!" I shout. "Come back! We need more carrots!"

Chapter Six

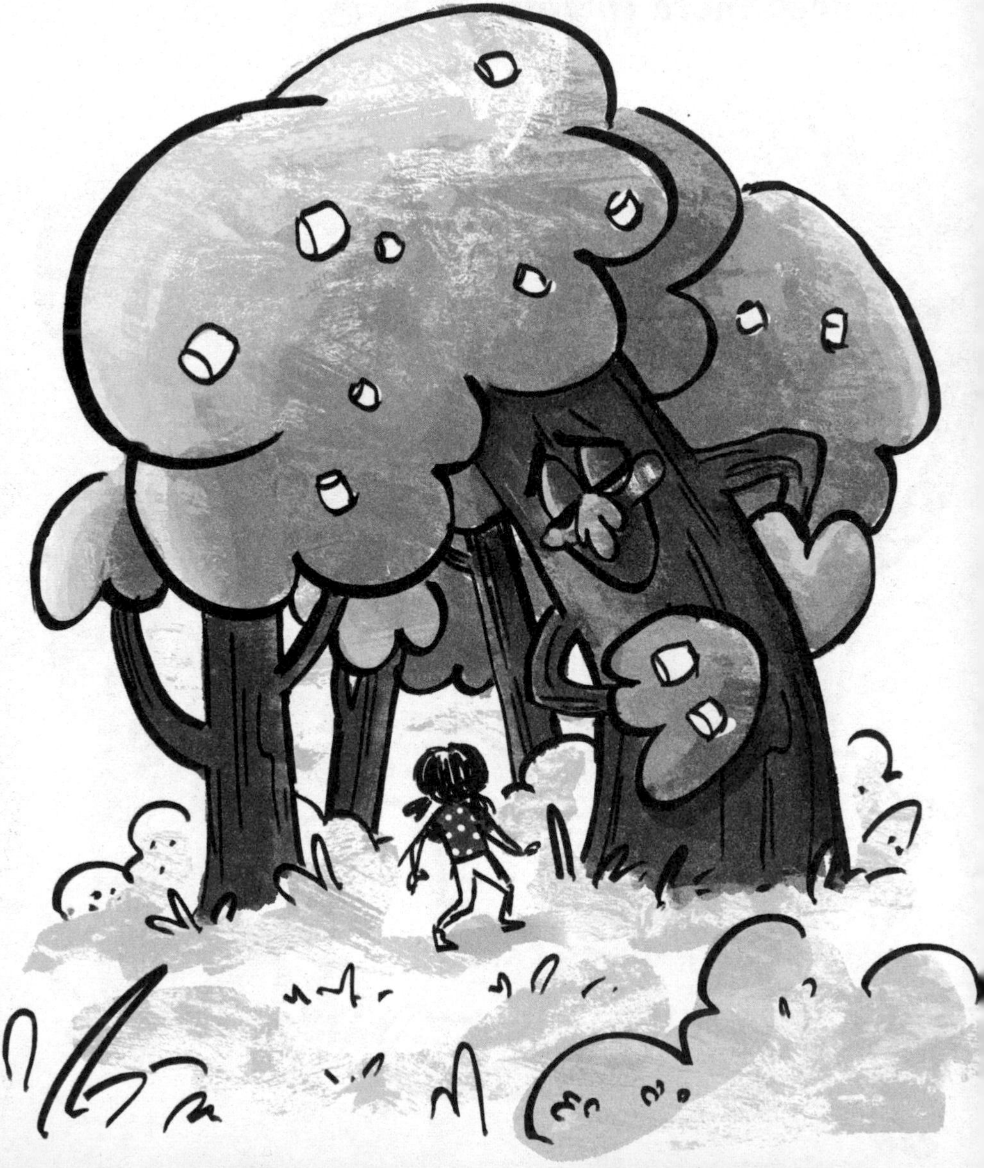

On the Right Track

"I would like to thank you for this crunchy treat, *I would*," says the tree standing in front of me. Then the *whole* tree bends over and *bows!*

"Hmm, would you happen to have another carrot, *you would?*" asks the tree to my left.

This is mind-boggling. *Are all the trees here alive?* I wonder.

Then Posey taps me on the arm. He's back with a basket full of carrots!

"I have some more," he says, offering the basket to me.

I take it and thank him.

"Anytime," Posey says. "And, by the way, I was only *pretending* to be afraid of the trees before."

I wink at my friend because we both know he's a *total* chicken.

Then the trees help themselves to the carrots.

"OM-NOM-NOM-NOM-NOM!" They munch happily. Flecks of carrot fly from their mouths and, it's a little bit gross. *Obviously.*

Then Posey clears his throat. He wants the trees' attention. He's feeling much more comfortable around them now.

"Since we've given you a treat," Posey begins, "would you please help us with something in return?"

The trees stop munching to listen.

"We were wondering," Posey goes on, "if you've seen a white bunny pass through your forest today. He's fluffy, he's fast, and he makes me very sneezy."

The trees look at one another and shrug their branches. Then the face of the one in front of me lights up.

"I know something that's white, fluffy, and fast, *I would*!" he says. Then the tree rustles his branches. Fluffy white marshmallows rain down on us like spongy Ping-Pong balls.

I scratch my head, because even though I *love* marshmallows, I am confused.

"How can a marshmallow be *fast*?" I ask.

But before they have time to answer, a whole new crop of marshmallows has formed on the trees' branches!

"Wow!" I say. "Your marshmallows grow super fast! But there's only one little problem. We're not looking for fast-growing marshmallows."

The trees stare at us blankly. Then I explain how Cutie Pie is a *rabbit*, though I'm not sure they understand.

They are *trees*, after all. In their world,
maybe bunnies are called yowberts?
Instead of giving me an answer, they
respond with a different question.

"You must be hungry, *you would!*"
they say. "You would have a marshmallow, *you would?*"

Hmm, come to think of it, Posey and I are a little bit hungry—so we accept their offer. Then we pick some marshmallows and pop them in our mouths. And YUMMA-LUMMA-TUMMY-TUM!

These marshmallows are so light, so fluffy, and oh so marsh-o-wowee-wow! *Obviously.*

I stuff my face until my cheeks puff out. Then I get right back to our pressing bunny mission but with my mouth full so the letter s sounds like *th*.

"Th-o can you help u-th find our loth-t bunny?" I ask.

"We would! *We would!*" The trees chant. Then they point to the forest floor with the tips of their branches.

"Just follow the footprints, *you would!*"

So Posey and I look at the ground. In between the marshmallows we spy what might be bunny tracks.

"But how can we be *sure* they're Cutie Pie's tracks?" I ask.

Posey drops to his knees and sniffs the footprints!

And before you can say *dust bunnies,*
he supergross sneezes. *"ACHOOO!"*

That settles it! These are
definitely Cutie Pie's tracks.

"Let's nab that bunny!"
I shout.

☆ CHAPTER SEVEN ☆

Things Get Hare-y

I've learned a few new things about bunnies today.

Number 1: Bunnies do *not* hop in a straight line—or, at least, Cutie Pie doesn't. His bunny tracks are curvy like spaghetti or else they go in circles. I'm pretty sure I've passed the same Marshmallow Tree five times *at least*!

Number 2: Bunnies can hop *far*.

Every time we turn a corner and I
think I'm going to see Cutie Pie's fluffy
tail and floppy ears, we just find *more*
bunny tracks. It's positively endless!

Then Posey yelps loudly and points
to something off in the distance. I look
in that direction, and there, over a hill

and far away, is something that looks like a bunny! *Could it be Cutie Pie? I ask myself.* It has to be!

"Let's go!" I cry, feeling a new burst of energy. But Posey has stopped to draw a bubble around his head with a pen.

"What in the World of Make-Believe are you drawing?" I ask.

Posey opens the part of the bubble covering his face.

"It's an astronaut's helmet," he says. "Now I can help rescue Cutie Pie without sneezing and scaring him away."

I hold up my hand, and we high-five because this is a very good Posey idea. Then Posey leaps into the air like a space guy, and he floats away after Cutie Pie.

Since he's taking the high road, I decide to take the low road. But first I pick up Posey's pen, which he left behind, and put it in my pocket for safekeeping.

Then I drop to the ground and crawl on my belly like a lizard. I don't want to scare that silly rabbit away either! Slowly, slowly I creep up on Cutie Pie. When I get close enough, I reach out my arms and wrap them around the bunny in a great big hug.

"Gotcha!" I cry, looking down at Cutie Pie.

Only it is *not* Cutie Pie.

It's not even a rabbit. Well, that's not completely true. It's a creature that seems to have a rabbit on top of its head. It literally has a *hare* on its *head*! Get it? Hair. Head.

And this creature is *not* alone. There's a whole bunch of these bunny-ish looking creatures that were hiding! And they are all glaring at me.

These not-bunnies are *not* happy with me.

Gulp.

☆ Chapter Eight ☆

Hop-Toppers

"Let go of my *hare!*" cries the squirmy creature, still wrapped in my arms.

I let the creature go free. He brushes himself off as the rest of his friends gather around me.

I apologize. "Oh my. I'm sorry. I thought you were a bunny—a bunny I'm looking for," I try to explain.

The one I captured scolds me.

"Well, you *should* be sorry!" he says. "You have ruined a *very* good hiding place."

I look around at all the little creatures staring at me.

"A very good hiding place?" I repeat. "I'm not sure what you mean.

I was just looking for my friend's bunny. Maybe you've seen him?"

Then the creatures all begin to talk at once.

"Bun . . . knee?" they question. "What is a bun . . . knee?"

I'm beginning to think bunnies may not exist in the WOM. The trees hadn't heard of them either. Then the creatures snap me back to attention.

"There's no time to talk!" one of the creatures warns, sniffing the air. "*Traygon* is coming!"

Posey floats down from the sky and lands in front of me.

"Where's Cutie Pie?" he asks.

Then I shake my head in disbelief, because seriously! *Read the room, dude!* *I'm surrounded by little creatures who are in a major tizzy.*

Finally Posey notices something's wrong and takes a closer look at the creatures.

"Hey! These are not rabbits," he declares. "They're Hop-Toppers!"

So that's what they're called, I think. The Hop-Toppers run this way and that. They seem to be looking for something, but I'm not sure what.

Then Posey covers his mouth with his hand.

"Shouldn't you be hiding?" he asks the Hop-Toppers. Then his voice drops to a whisper. "What about *Traygon?*"

The very word "Traygon" sets the Hop-Toppers off again. They cry and squeal and scurry this way and that. One of the Hop-Toppers complains about me to Posey.

"Well, your friend gave away our hiding spot!" she says. "And now we have to find another one!"

Posey turns to me and shakes his head gravely. "You shouldn't have done that," he says. "Hiding spots are very important to Hop-Toppers because Traygon is *always* chasing them."

I throw my hands up in the air. "How am I supposed to know that, Posey?" I ask. "And who is *Traygon?*"

As soon as I say the name, a dark shadow spreads over all of us until there's no more sun in the sky.

I swallow hard.

"Um, Posey?" I whisper. "Does Traygon have blue scales, black wings, pointy teeth, yellow eyes, and a spiny back like a dragon?"

Posey nods like crazy. "She does! How'd you know?" he asks in surprise. "In fact, she *is* a dragon, which means she also breathes fire. We definitely need to be on the lookout."

I point behind Posey and cry, "In that case . . . LOOK OUT!"

Chapter Nine

Cracking Up

I thought Cutie Pie was fast, but the Hop-Toppers split faster than a banana at an ice-cream shop!

"*GRRROOAAR!*"

Traygon roars the roariest roar I have ever heard. Even Marshmallow Trees pull up their roots and run away. I would bet a thousand peanut butter cups this dragon is *not* friendly.

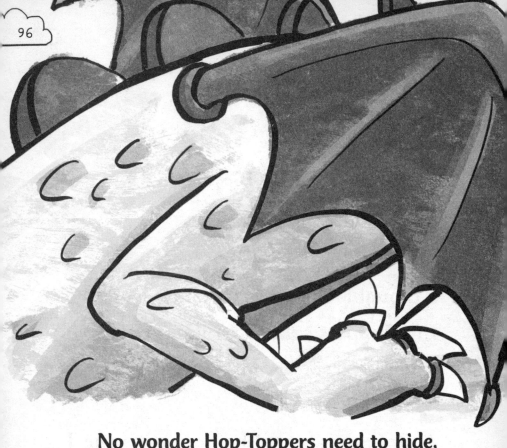

No wonder Hop-Toppers need to hide.

I look for somewhere to hide too, but now that the trees are all gone, Posey and I are left standing in the middle of a bare field. There is nothing

between us and Traygon, and she's getting closer by the second!

"Posey," I whisper, "we need to draw a door back to the real world *right now*. It's our only way out!"

Posey takes off his special space helmet and reaches into his pockets, looking for his pen. He pulls out a watermelon, a rubber snake, a fortune cookie, a few leftover marshmallows, a floor lamp, some mustard packets, and his new pet rock, Shelly.

Then he places Shelly on his head, and I think, *This is no time for games!*

"Posey!" I cry. "Where is your pen?"

Posey crinkles his forehead. "Oh no. I lost it!"

And that's when I remember—he didn't lose the pen. *I* have it!

"*GRRRROOOAAAR!*" Traygon roars again. The ground shake-shake-shakes beneath us.

I quickly shove my hand into my pocket and pull out the pen, but it's too late. Traygon is standing *right* over us, and I'm pretty sure we are about to be eaten or burned to a crisp.

Then, out of the corner of my eye, I spy Cutie Pie climbing up Posey's back!

"There you are!" I shout, but who cares? We are total goners! Is this what happens when you babysit your best friend's bunny?

Suddenly Lily's fluffy little Cutie Pie nudges Shelly the rock right off the top of Posey's head, and the rock tips straight toward Traygon!

"Shelly!" Posey screams.

Traygon catches the rock in her claws just as I lunge for Cutie Pie. Because I *know* what happens when Posey's near Cutie Pie.

But I'm not fast enough.

"ACHOOO!"

Globs of glitter snot spray every-where. Traygon and Shelly get the worst of it. The dragon squints her

eyes and shakes her head to get rid
of the gooey sparkle slime. And then,
for a brief moment, the WOM is quiet,
except for a strange cracking noise.

"Criiick! Craaack! Criiick!"

Uh-oh. Something's happening to Shelly. It looks like she's coming apart! Then I realize Shelly's not a rock! *She's an egg!* She must be Traygon's dragon egg! And she's hatching!

Pieces of shell drop to the ground, and there, in Traygon's arms, is the world's cutest baby dragon. Traygon sighs and looks at us thankfully. Then she spreads her enormous wings and flies away with her baby.

Posey and I look at each other with our mouths hanging open.

"Well, that's not something you see every day," Posey says. "Even in the World of Make-Believe!"

Chapter Ten

My Secret Is Safe

"I have to go home!" I say, handing the pen back to Posey.

He draws a door to the Real World. "I better stay here," he says, sniffling and pointing at Cutie Pie.

I give my imaginary friend a huge air hug so he doesn't sneeze. Then I step back into the real world just as Lily bursts through my bedroom door.

Whew. Talk about good timing!

"Here are the bunny treats and toys!" Lily says, opening her bag and pulling out a pack of tree-shaped treats. "I don't know why, but these are Cutie Pie's favorite. Oh, and here's his favorite toy," she adds, handing me a tiny stuffed dragon.

I turn the tiny dragon over in my hand. *Wow, it looks so much like Traygon!* It makes me wonder, *Did Cutie Pie know where he was going today? Maybe he wanted to see a real dragon.*

I watch Lily snuggle her face into her bunny's fur.

"I'm going to miss you so much, Cutie Pie!" she whispers, and I can tell she means it.

"Thanks again, Daisy," she says, handing Cutie Pie back to me. Then she looks around my glitter-tastic room, and I hold my breath. This is it. Game over. Lily is going to know something is up!

But instead, she asks, "Hey, did you redecorate? Your room looks . . . brighter."

"No," I say with a giggle. "I think Cutie Pie brightens up the place."

Lily nods, and then she gives me and Cutie Pie a big hug before racing back to her car.

Once she's gone, I hold Cutie Pie up to my face.

"I know you're just a fluffy bunny who loves dragons and doesn't talk, but could you please promise to never *ever* tell Lily about what happened today?"

Then guess what! That hare-brained bunny totally winks at me. And I sigh a great sigh of relief.

Because I know my secret is safe with Cutie Pie.

Check out Daisy Dreamer's next adventure!

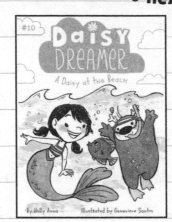

"Wow! You look beachy cool, Daisy Dreamer!" I say to the me in the mirror. I am wearing my favorite bathing suit. It has colorful stripes and *spaghetti* straps. But not *real* spaghetti. *Obviously.*

Why am I dressed in a bathing suit? Because today I'm going to the beach!

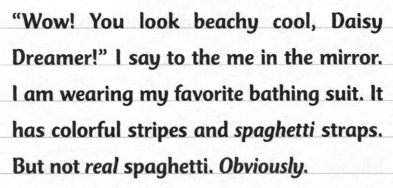

Excerpt from *A Daisy at the Beach*

I sway my hips and pretend to be a hula girl, moving my arms from left to right. I can almost hear the music playing, but my cat, Sir Pounce, looks at me like I'm a weirdo.

Enough hula dancing for now! Time to pack my beach bag. I have a super-long list of things to take to the beach:

Mermaid beach towel.
Sparkly, strawberry-scented sunscreen.
Heart-shaped movie star sunglasses.
Over-the-rainbow striped folding
    beach chair.

Boogie woogie boogie board.

Hmmm. I tap my head thought-fully. Did I forget anything? Then I snap my fingers and write down:

Starfish sand buckets.
Neon green and yellow shovels.
Swim goggles.
Book.

And oh yeah! One more thing! I race out of my bedroom and lean over the railing. "MOM!" I shout at the top of my lungs. "Do you have my beach umbrella?" I wait for an answer.

"All packed, honey!" Mom shouts back.

Excerpt from *A Daisy at the Beach*